Win the Race!

Illustrated by The Artful Doodlers

Random House New York
Thomas the Tank Engine & Friends™

CREATED BY BRITT ALLCROFT

Based on The Railway Series by The Reverend W Awdry. © 2010 Gullane (Thomas) LLC.
Thomas the Tank Engine & Friends and Thomas & Friends are trademarks of Gullane (Thomas) Limited.
HIT and the HIT Entertainment logo are trademarks of HIT Entertainment Limited.
All rights reserved. Published in the United States by Random House Children's Books, a division of Random House, Inc., 1745 Broadway,
New York, NY 10019, and in Canada by Random House of Canada Limited, Toronto. Step into Reading, Random House, and the
Random House colophon are registered trademarks of Random House, Inc.
www.stepintoreading.com   www.randomhouse.com/kids   www.thomasandfriends.com

Educators and librarians, for a variety of teaching tools, visit us at
www.randomhouse.com/teachers
ISBN: 978-0-375-85368-5   MANUFACTURED IN CHINA

HiT entertainment

Thomas and James will have a race.

Will James win?

Will Thomas win?

Sir Topham Hatt has a big bell.

He will ring the bell.

He will yell go!

"Go!"

There they go!

Thomas and James race

up the hill.

They will go up

to the top of the hill.

Will Thomas win?

Will James win?

They are fast trains.

Where are Thomas and James?

There they are!

They are in the woods.

It looks like Thomas will win.

Look!

There goes James.

James can fill the gap.

It looks like James will win.

Will James win?

Will Thomas win?

Here is the line.

It is a tie!

They both win.